Thanksgiving

A Level Two Reader

By Cynthia Klingel and Robert B. Noyed

The
Child's
World®

Thanksgiving is a holiday in the United States. It takes place on the fourth Thursday in November.

The Pilgrims held the first

Thanksgiving. That was

almost 400 years ago!

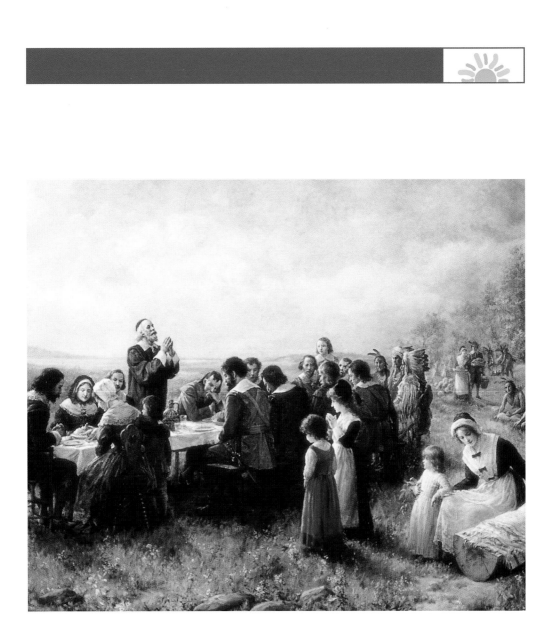

The Pilgrims had come to America from another country. They worked hard in their new country.

Native Americans helped
the Pilgrims. They taught
them how to plant corn
and beans.

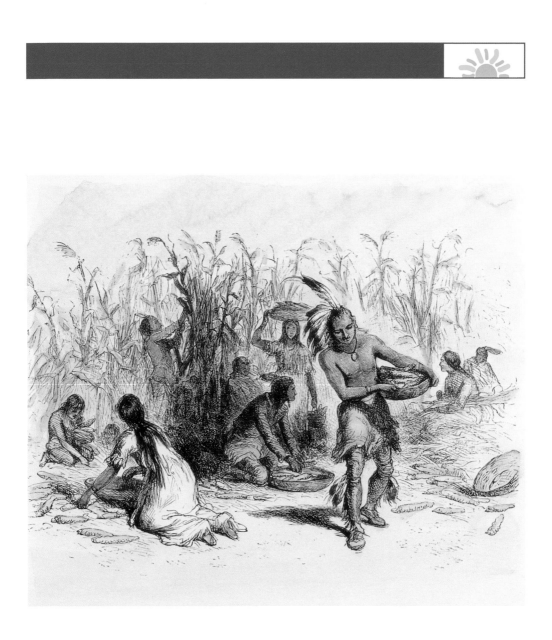

The Pilgrims were thankful for their new life. At the end of the summer, they had food in their gardens.

In the fall, the Pilgrims had a large feast. They had many reasons to give thanks.

Today, many people still have a special meal on Thanksgiving. They eat many kinds of good food.

Turkey is a favorite food on Thanksgiving. The turkey looks and smells so tasty.

Many people like to eat pumpkin pie on Thanksgiving. Don't eat too much!

Thanksgiving is a time to be with family and friends. Thanksgiving is a time to give thanks for what we have.

Index

To Find Out More

Books

Bauer, Caroline Feller. *Thanksgiving Stories and Poems.* New York: HarperCollins, 1994.

Merrick, Patrick. *Thanksgiving Turkeys.* Chanhassen, Minn.: Child's World, 2000.

Roop, Peter. *Let's Celebrate Thanksgiving.* Brookfield, Conn.: Millbrook Press, 1999.

Web Sites

Celebrate! Holidays in the U.S.A.: Thanksgiving
http://www.usis.usemb.se/Holidays/celebrate/thanksgi.html
For an article about Thanksgiving from a U.S. embassy.

22

Note to Parents and Educators

Welcome to Wonder Books®! These books provide text at three different levels for beginning readers to practice and strengthen their reading skills. Additionally, the use of nonfiction text provides readers the valuable opportunity to *read to learn*, not just to learn to read.

These leveled readers allow children to choose books at their level of reading confidence and performance. Nonfiction Level One books offer beginning readers simple language, word choice, and sentence structure as well as a word list. Nonfiction Level Two books feature slightly more difficult vocabulary, longer sentences, and longer total text. In the back of each Nonfiction Level Two book are an index and a list of books and Web sites for finding out more information. Nonfiction Level Three books continue to extend word choice and length of text. In the back of each Nonfiction Level Three book are a glossary, an index, and a list of books and Web sites for further research.

State and national standards in reading and language arts emphasize using nonfiction at all levels of reading development. Wonder Books® fill the historical void in nonfiction material for primary grade readers with the additional benefit of a leveled text.

About the Authors

Cynthia Klingel has worked as a high school English teacher and an elementary school teacher. She is currently the curriculum director for a Minnesota school district. Cynthia lives with her family in Mankato, Minnesota.

Robert B. Noyed started his career as a newspaper reporter. Since then, he has worked in school communications and public relations at the state and national level. Robert lives with his family in Brooklyn Center, Minnesota.

Published by The Child's World®, Inc.
PO Box 326
Chanhassen, MN 55317-0326
800-599-READ
www.childsworld.com

Photo Credits
© 2003 David Young-Wolff/Stone: cover, 14, 21
© Martha McBride/Unicorn Stock Photos: 17
© N. Carter/North Wind Pictures: 10
© North Wind Pictures: 9
© Photri, Inc.: 5
© Rita Maas/Imagebank: 2
© Rick Barrentine/CORBIS: 18
© Stock Montage, Inc.: 6, 13

Project Coordination: Editorial Directions, Inc.
Photo Research: Alice K. Flanagan

Library of Congress Cataloging-in-Publication Data
Klingel, Cynthia Fitterer.
Thanksgiving / by Cynthia Klingel and Robert B. Noyed.
    p. cm. — (Wonder books)
Includes bibliographical references and index.
ISBN 1-56766-956-5 (lib. bdg. : alk. paper)
1. Thanksgiving Day—Juvenile literature.
[1. Thanksgiving Day. 2. Holidays.]
I. Noyed, Robert B. II. Title. III. Wonder books
(Chanhassen, Minn.)
GT4975 .K55 2001
394.2649—dc21
                                00-011363

24